...NG AT THE STARS

Then a voice called out.

'Play *Open Book* again!'

Layla smiled. 'I'm glad you liked it,' she said.

'Play it again! All your other songs are rubbish!'

Layla didn't know what to say. She'd never had a heckler before. She tried to make out where his voice was coming from. There were too many people for her to tell.

'See what you think of this one,' she said. 'This is my last song.'

'Good thing too!'

Layla got through the last song. The applause was loud. A few people even shouted out for an encore. But the day was ruined.

Look out for other exciting stories
in the *Shades* series:

SHOUTING AT THE STARS

David Belbin

Evans

In memory of Kevin Coyne,
singer-songwriter 1944-2004

Published by Evans Brothers Limited
2A Portman Mansions
Chiltern St
London W1U 6NR

First published in 2005

British Library Cataloguing in Publication Data
Belbin, David
   Shouting at the stars. - (Shades)
   1. Stalking - Fiction 2. Stalking victims - Fiction 3. Singers
   - Fiction 4. Stalkers - Fiction 5. Suspense fiction 6. Young
   adult fiction
   I. Title
   823. 9'14 [J]

   ISBN-10: 023752923 8

13-digit ISBN (from January 2007) 978 0 237 52923 9

Series Editor: David Orme
Editor: Julia Moffatt
Designer: Rob Walster

Prologue

It was Layla's first press interview. The photos came first. They took longer than the questions.

'Are you really nineteen?' the reporter asked. 'You look younger.'

'I look young for my age,' Layla said.

'Tell me about yourself.'

'I'm an only child. I grew up in a small

town. When I got a guitar, girls at school teased me. I played all the time and was too busy to have boyfriends.'

'But now you have a recording deal,' the reporter said. 'And do you have a boyfriend?'

'None of your business,' Layla said. She didn't want to tell the world that she'd never had a boyfriend. Not a serious one.

'What's your magazine called?' she asked.

Someone called out, 'We're ready for you now.'

'Good luck with the show,' the reporter said.

Layla was nervous. She had played small shows before. She'd played to hundreds, as the support act. But this was her first festival. Thousands would be watching. All she had were her voice, her songs and one guitar. Her manager pushed her on to the stage.

When she picked up her guitar, Layla's confidence returned. There was a warm breeze. The faces in the crowd seemed to be smiling. She began with the song that would be her first single. It was called *Open Book*.

Now my heart's an open book, she sang.

Take a look. Go on, take a look.

She finished to a big cheer. The crowd were on her side. The next four songs went well. She only had one more to do. She stopped to retune one of her guitar strings. The crowd was quiet. Then a voice called out.

'Play *Open Book* again!'

Layla smiled. 'I'm glad you liked it,' she said.

'Play it again! All your other songs are rubbish!'

Layla didn't know what to say. She'd never had a heckler before. She tried to make out where his voice was coming from. There were too many people for her to tell.

'See what you think of this one,' she said.

'This is my last song.'

'Good thing too!'

Layla got through the last song. The applause was loud. A few people even shouted out for an encore. But the day was ruined.

Chapter One

The interview was in *New Lad* magazine.
Layla wished she'd not worn such a low-cut
top. The photo made her look cheap. Never
mind. Her single was a hit. Not a big one,
but big enough. The video made Layla look
sexy, mysterious. The label spent a fortune
to produce and advertise her album.

When the album came out, Layla began

her first headlining tour. Layla was to play in small theatres, clubs and universities. The crowds weren't huge, but she never had less than a hundred people. It was winter. For each gig, she wore a long dress and a cardigan. When it got hot on stage, she took off the cardigan.

The heckler appeared at the second show, in Leeds. Layla had just taken off her cardigan.

'Take the rest of your clothes off!' he yelled.

'That's not funny,' Layla said, looking around. The lights were bright. She couldn't see where the voice was coming from.

'Everyone saw you in *New Lad* magazine!'

A few people in the hall shushed the heckler.

'We all make mistakes,' Layla muttered. She began the next song.

'You're a fake!' the heckler called out.

Layla ignored him. For the rest of the set, Layla expected the heckler to call out again. He didn't, but it was too late for her to recover. Her singing was so-so, but her guitar-playing was rubbish.

'This is my last song,' she said after only forty minutes.

'It'd better be *Open Book*,' the heckler yelled. 'It's your only good song. Remember, I told you before!'

'I thought your voice was familiar,' Layla said.

She played *Open Book*. As she left the stage, the crowd called for an encore. Layla's manager wasn't there, so she spoke to the woman from the Students' Union.

'Can you try to find the guy who was calling out? I'd like to speak to him.'

'Are you sure?'

'Just get him,' she said.

Layla might be small, thin and young looking, but she was tough. You had to be, to make it in this business. She went back on stage. When the applause died down, she waited for the heckler to shout out. But he didn't.

'We couldn't find him,' said the student afterwards. 'I asked around, but he was gone.'

'Did anybody say what he looked like?' Layla asked.

'Just a young guy. Your age, maybe. I wouldn't worry.'

'He'll be back,' Layla said.

'What's he going to do? Follow you from city to city?'

The thought made Layla shiver.

Her next show was at The Maze in Nottingham. The Maze was at the back of a pub. It was the smallest venue on the tour. People entered through the pub, but Layla couldn't get in that way. There was no ramp for her wheelchair. She had to go in through the fire escape entry at the back.

The place was full. She could see the faces of all the people in front of her. There were dozens more, at the side and by the bar. She couldn't see them properly. But there was no heckler. The gig was wonderful, her best yet.

When the show was over, she signed some autographs. A young man, about her age, held out a copy of *New Lad*.

'I don't want to sign that,' she said.

'Why not? You look great in it.' He opened the magazine at her picture. 'Please?'

Layla gave in. 'What do you want me to write?' she asked.

'How about, *For Gary, with love?*'

Layla covered her chest with words.

'Magic! I'm going to put it on the wall above my bed in my hall of residence.'

She looked at Gary. He had long hair and a thin face with a few spots. He wasn't bad looking. A year ago, if he'd asked her out, she would have said "yes".

'Are you at university here?' she asked.

'No. Derby. I came by train. I'm going to see you in Birmingham too. I thought you were great at that festival in Leicester.'

'Thanks a lot,' she said, before speaking to the next in line. The lad was following her around. He had been at the festival. Was he the heckler? If he was, why would he be so nice to her? And why hadn't he called out tonight?

Chapter Two

Birmingham Town Hall had reserved seats. Before she went on, Layla asked her manager, Ben, to keep an eye out.

'You won't get a heckler here,' Ben said. 'It's far too posh.'

'Just in case,' Layla said.

She was being paranoid. This was the fifth show on the tour. The heckler had only been at one of them. She knew Gary from Derby was coming tonight. So what? Why would he tell her if he was going to heckle?

She spotted Gary after the third song. He was in the second row, and kept smiling. Halfway through, he called out for a new song, one that wasn't on the album. He was a big fan, that was all. He liked the music. Layla sang the song for him.

'Don't give up your day job,' a voice called out when the song finished. The shout seemed to come from near the front. It might be Gary. She couldn't be sure.

'This *is* my day job,' she said. 'Since you liked that so much, here's another new one.'

There were some warm chuckles from the audience. She had dealt with the heckler. Was it the guy from Leeds and Leicester? She wasn't sure.

The rest of the show went well. Layla

finished with *Open Book*. As she played the opening chords, a voice called out.

'Take your cardy off!'

'What?' Layla stopped the song.

'Take it off!' the voice yelled. 'You look better without it on.' There were lots of shushing noises. Layla was sure it was the voice from before. She looked at Gary in the second row. Was it him? His mouth was closed now.

'It's a little cold for that,' she said. 'This is my last song. Thanks for coming.'

'Thanks for nothing!' the voice called back. Layla was looking at her guitar strings and didn't see who it was.

Layla got through *Open Book*, then left the stage.

'Did you see him?' she asked Ben.

'I didn't get a good look at the heckler, but I know where he's sitting.'

'Corner him after the show, please,' she said. 'Bring him to talk to me.'

'If you insist,' Ben said.

She returned to play an encore. Nobody called out. Maybe Layla had overreacted when she asked to meet the guy. But she wanted to stop this. She didn't want to worry about dealing with the heckler every time she played a gig.

'Did you find him?' she asked Ben once she was offstage.

'Yes. He agreed to meet you when you've finished signing CDs.'

'What does he look like?'

'Ordinary. Twenty or so. Medium height, longish fair hair.'

It sounded like Gary.

'Did you ask him why he did it?' Layla asked.

'No. He's a mumbler. He just kept

staring at the floor.'

Layla went to the stall that was selling CDs. She had her photo taken with fans. The last person in line was Gary from Derby. He grinned.

'You again,' she said. She was sorry he was the heckler.

Gary held out a new CD for her to sign.

'Didn't you have this already?' she asked.

'I've got another copy at home, but I'll give it to somebody for Christmas.'

'Why do you do it, Gary?'

'Do what?'

'What you're doing?'

'You mean, follow you around? Because I think you're great. Your songs, they really get to me. I made sure I was last in line so I'd have more time to talk to you.'

'But the calling out? "Get your cardy off".'

Gary looked stunned. 'You think that's me?

I saw that guy, in the row behind me. He was at Leeds, too. He's a creep. The world is full of creeps. He doesn't sound anything like me. I can't believe you thought…'

Gary shook his head, then walked off without another word. He'd left his CD behind.

'Sorry,' Layla called, but he didn't seem to hear.

Ben returned. 'Sorry,' he said. 'The heckler left ten minutes ago. I tried to make him stay but he pushed his way out.'

Chapter Three

The next day began badly. Layla was
travelling to London alone. Ben had to
see one of his other artists. Layla had a
reserved space on the train to London but
several people had put their bags in it. The
train staff said it wasn't their job to move
them. So Layla had to travel in the guard's
van, just like she did when she was a child.

Her chair faced the wall. When nobody was around, she had a little cry.

'Pull yourself together!' she told herself. She'd come too far to let one nutter put her off. Layla got a pen and notebook out. She began to write the words to a song. Some days, words came easily. This was one of those days.

After a while, Layla could hear a melody in her head. It drove the words along. The song wasn't about her heckler. It was about what made the heckler what he was. In the story she made up, the heckler lost his girlfriend to a rock star. The only thing that made him feel good was shouting at famous people. So he went to gigs, where he mocked whoever was on stage.

Layla wrote three verses before the train got to London. She didn't know how to end the story. It didn't matter. She couldn't play the song live until she got rid of her own heckler.

In London, she met with her record company.

'Ben feels bad he can't be at all your shows,' the label boss said. 'He says there's some creep following you around. We think you need somebody with you all the time.'

'It's nothing to worry about,' Layla said.

'Maybe not, Layla. But let's face it, you can't run away if somebody tries to attack you.'

Layla didn't argue. The label had signed her after seeing a photo and hearing a demo CD. They didn't back out when they found she was in a chair and had had a nervous breakdown five years ago. It was their job to protect her.

'We're hiring you a personal assistant,' the boss said. 'I want you to meet Mick.'

A guy in a leather bomber jacket came in. He had wide shoulders, a shaved head and a rose tattoo on his arm. Layla gave him an awkward smile.

'Mick's going to be with you 24-7 when you're on tour. He'll carry stuff and watch out for creeps. With him around, you'll have nothing to worry about.'

'Won't I?' Layla asked. 'If I've got nothing to worry about, why do I need a bodyguard?'

'For peace of mind. He starts next week.'

Layla was playing a dozen gigs as the support act to a big American band. This was the first time she'd played huge halls. The audiences were friendly. Each night, more than half of the crowd came early to hear her play. Hardly anybody walked out. Layla enjoyed herself. There was no heckler.

The tickets must be too expensive for him.

Her last night on the tour was at the Birmingham NEC. Layla decided to play her new song. After all, the heckler wouldn't be there. Even if he was, the place was so big, nobody would be able to hear him.

'This is a new song,' Layla told the crowd. 'It's about a guy who goes to gigs so that he can get in the spotlight himself. It's called *Shouting at the Stars*.'

As she sang, Layla could sense an extra buzz in the air. After two verses, the crowd were really enjoying it. The arena was still, silent. Then came the call.

'You're no star!'

Flustered, Layla repeated the second verse. As soon as she ended it, the guy called out again.

'Are you saying I'm a sicko?'

Out of the corner of her eye, Layla made

out Mick, walking down one wide aisle, then the other. He was looking for the heckler. She couldn't keep her mind on the song. So she stopped playing.

'Sorry,' she said. 'Looks like that one isn't ready yet. Here's another one from my album.'

She closed her eyes as she sang *Talking to No-one*. When she finished, the applause was warm and the hall went quiet. Her time was nearly up.

'This is my last number. Some of you might know this one,' she said.

'Some of us might want to forget it,' the heckler yelled. Layla shuddered. Then she played *Open Book*.

Backstage, everyone said she'd been excellent.

'You were great,' said the lead singer of the headline band. 'Don't let hecklers put you off. We all get them.'

'You too?' Layla asked.

'Louder and drunker than yours. Come to think of it, yours didn't sound drunk. I like that song you started to sing. Make sure you record it.'

'I will,' Layla said.

Mick came in.

'Did you find him?' Layla asked.

Mick shook his head. 'I asked around. I found where he was sitting. Seems he took an empty seat near the front. It belonged to someone who hadn't arrived yet. He left as soon as you finished. Now he's probably at the back somewhere.'

'Or he's gone home maybe,' Layla said. 'Never mind.'

'He spoiled your show,' Mick said. 'It's my job to catch him. I've got to tell him what's what.'

'I want to talk to him,' Layla said. 'There must be a way to make him understand how he puts me off.'

'There's only one kind of language people like him understand,' Mick said, his hand in a fist.

Chapter Four

Layla's first European tour was in early
spring. She was glad to be on the road again.
Her parents said she worked too hard and
looked strained. But Layla missed playing
live. To her surprise, she also missed Mick.
He looked hard, but it was an act. He was
smart and gentle. She'd never had a bloke
come so close before. They had a laugh.

Layla had rewritten her song about the heckler, *Shouting at the Stars*. She played it every night in the small halls of Munich, Vienna and Berlin. The song always went down well. On mainland Europe, the only people who shouted out were the ones requesting songs.

'Soon you'll be too big to tour like this,' Mick said. 'You'll need a band with a sound big enough for arenas.'

'I don't think so,' Layla told him. 'We don't all want to be huge stars. I'd be happy if things stayed like this.'

'Me too,' Mick said, with a warm glint in his eye. Layla smiled back. It was strange that she fancied someone she used to think was ugly. But she did.

By now, Layla should have learnt that things never stay the same. Her third single, *The World is Full of Fools*, turned out to be a big hit. It went to number one in six countries, including the UK. After Layla's gig in Milan, Ben, her manager, rang up. The record company wanted her to tour the UK again.

'I've done two UK tours in the last six months,' she told Ben on the phone. 'Can't it wait until autumn?'

'Interview requests are pouring in. If you tour in May, I promise you, your album will sell a million. Then you can play a few festivals and take the rest of the summer off.'

'I don't know if I can wait until July for a break.'

'Do you want to be a big star, or not? What else have you been working for?'

Layla backed down. 'I'll be OK. I'm just tired tonight.'

'Have you had your medical check-up?'

'Yes, and I'm getting plenty of exercise.

You don't need to worry about my health.'

When she put the phone down, Layla began to cry. There was a knock on the door. It was Mick. He'd come to say goodnight.

'What's wrong?' he asked.

Layla wiped her eyes.

'Sorry to be a wimp,' she said. 'All this work is never ending.'

'You must miss your family and friends,' Mick said.

Layla didn't reply. Her friends weren't the same since she became a star. They didn't know how to treat her. Even her mum and dad didn't know how to behave around her.

Mick sat down on the bed next to Layla.

'Is there anything I can do to help?' he asked.

'Just hold me,' she said.

Chapter Five

The last date on Layla's European tour was in Dublin.

'I'm going to play a few new songs tonight,' she told the crowd. She sang *So Strange*, a song she'd written for Mick. They were keeping their relationship secret.

Layla had a personal stylist and make-up expert. Other stars came to see her play.

One even asked her out. But Layla was happier watching movies with Mick than hanging out with big stars.

'Here's another new one,' she said. 'It was inspired by something that happened to me on my first tour.'

She began the song.

Just another small town dreamer
She broke his heart the first time out
Turned him into a screw-loose schemer
The band plays and he starts to shout

'Like this?' called a voice from the stalls. Layla ignored it. When she began the second verse, he shouted over her words.

'You know nothing about me! Nothing!'

There were hissing noises in the crowd. People were looking round to see who was making the fuss. Layla could see Mick hurrying down the centre aisle, trying to spot the heckler. But she wasn't going to let him stop her tonight. She sang the third verse, then the fourth. The heckler stopped shouting. She had won. When she finished the song, the applause was the loudest of the evening.

'Did you find him?' she asked Mick afterwards.

He shook his head. 'I couldn't locate where he was sitting. He must have gone quiet as soon as he saw me coming. I tried to ask who he was. But you were singing. People kept telling me to shut up. I asked afterwards. People who were near him said he left in a hurry. He looked very ordinary, they said.'

'I should have remembered how close we are to the UK,' Layla said. 'I shouldn't have played that song.'

'Why not? It's one of your best ones. You should play it every night. We'll find out who he is. Ben says we can get a lawyer to stop him coming to your gigs.'

'What for?' Layla asked. 'Shouting out a few times?'

She'd not been looking forward to the UK tour. Now she dreaded it.

'I'll stop him,' Mick promised.

Chapter Six

The UK tour sold out as soon as tickets went on sale. Layla had her own bus. The hotels were better than before. Yet success was less fun than she'd hoped. Layla didn't need to do this tour. Her album was already at number one.

Ben came along for the first show. 'The festivals all want you,' he said. 'You'll be on the main stage at Glastonbury. Then there's Reading, and T in the Park.'

'I don't want to do festivals,' she said. 'I don't want to play halls any bigger than I am tonight.'

She was playing at the Royal Concert Hall in Nottingham. Seven months ago, she'd played to a hundred people at the back of a pub up the hill. Tonight, there would be more than two thousand, just to see her. It was a steep climb.

'Things will slow down soon,' Ben promised. 'We're going to add one big gig to finish off the tour.'

'Where?' Layla asked.

'Surprise. You'll be pleased, I promise.'

Layla was nervous before she took to the stage. She'd not been sleeping well. Her doctor offered her sedatives.

'No thanks,' Layla said. 'I don't want to take anything that might make me lose my edge.'

'Everybody uses something,' the doctor told her. 'There's no shame in it.'

'I'm not ashamed of anything,' Layla told the doctor. 'I'm just tired. I need a holiday.'

'Are you still hearing voices?'

'How do you mean?'

'Ben mentioned how upset you get by these hecklers at your concerts. And it says in your notes that a similar thing happened when you were fourteen. You heard voices in your head.'

'I'm not imagining it this time. It's only one heckler. He follows me around.'

'A young woman like you attracts all sorts of strange men. It's probably more than one. You mustn't take things like that seriously. You must learn to block them out.'

Layla ignored the word *them*. 'How can I?' she asked.

'If you ignore people, they tend to go away.'

'That's your advice? *Ignore him.*'

'That's right. Ignore them and they'll go away.'

Mick and Ben were in the Royal Concert Hall, one standing at each side. There was no aisle down the middle. If the heckler was in the stalls, they would see him and make sure he didn't escape. The hall also had a circle and a balcony upstairs. But the heckler always sat in the stalls.

Layla sang a lot of new songs. The show wasn't long enough otherwise. In halls like this, you had to play for an hour-and-a-half. Otherwise, people didn't think they'd got their money's worth. Ben said Layla had to talk more between the songs. She had to become an entertainer.

'Here's another one you won't know,' she told the crowd. 'This is called *Blame it on the Night.*'

'I blame you for singing it!' A familiar voice yelled. He was back. Layla ignored him and began the song. She wasn't going to let the heckler get the better of her.

'Play the old stuff,' he yelled after the new song. 'Play stuff we know!'

'Patience,' Layla said. 'I wasn't going to play this song, but since we have a heckler here anyway…'

'I paid my money like everyone else!' the heckler yelled. People began to shush loudly. Others yelled, 'Get out!'

'If you want to leave now, I'll instruct my manager to give you a full refund at the door,' Layla said. 'I'm sure everyone else would enjoy the show more.'

There was a huge round of applause. Layla waited for the heckler to speak again, but he didn't.

'This song's called *Shouting at the Stars*. It's going to be the title song of my next album.'

That night Layla performed the song so well, she wished the night had been recorded. When it was over, she waited for the heckler to call out. He didn't. Had she beaten him, or had Ben and Mick removed him from the hall?

The rest of the show was like a dream. It was the best concert she'd ever given.

'We couldn't get near him,' Mick explained after the show. 'He was sitting right in the middle, on the sixth row. On his own, as far as I could tell.'

'I tried to talk to him afterwards,' Ben said. 'I told him you wanted a word with him. But he pushed past me.'

'I would have stopped him,' Mick said. 'Only, I know you don't want any violence. I tried to grab him, but there were lots of people around. I did get this, though.'

He handed her his phone. He'd taken a photo on it. There was her heckler, leaving the hall. He had a hood on his head. Even so, she could see his long nose, his narrow chin. He had a dull, far-away look in his eyes. At least now she was certain he wasn't Gary from Derby. As far as she knew, Gary hadn't been to a show since Birmingham.

'If he shows up again,' Mick said, 'I'll kill him.'

Chapter Six

The photograph on the phone haunted Layla. Who was the heckler? Why did he spend so much money coming to see her?

She dreamt about meeting the heckler. On stage, when she sang the song about him, she waited for him to shout out. He didn't.

'You've seen him off,' Mick said.

But she hadn't. At the fourth show of the tour, in Leeds, he was there again. He wasn't as loud this time. His seat must be further back. He kept calling out for *Open Book*, which she always saved for the encore.

'I'll get to it,' Layla said.

'Play it now!'

'Did you find him?' Layla asked after the show.

'No,' Mick said. 'I'm not even sure it *was* him this time.'

The next night, in Manchester, he was there again. Layla had decided not to play *Shouting at the Stars*. People still called out for it. They had seen her sing the song or heard it on a fan recording. Everyone said it was her best song. Better than *Open Book*. Better than her number one.

'Go on, play it!' yelled the voice she dreaded. 'I don't mind. In fact, I'm flattered!'

'You're the reason I don't sing it,' Layla said.

'I'm the reason you wrote it!'

Layla couldn't argue with that. She sang the song, badly. After that, he shut up.

'Why didn't you catch him?' she asked Mick in the hotel.

'I couldn't see where he was,' Mick said. 'The thing is, people know about the heckler. Lots of them have heard the song. They talk about the story all the time on the internet. It could be someone pretending to be him.'

'I know his voice,' Layla said. 'Tonight it was him.'

'There's only one way in and out of tomorrow night's show,' Mick said. 'If he's there, I'll catch him.'

'You'd better.'

'Come on,' he told her. 'Time for bed.'

'Not yet,' Layla said. 'I want to sit and think for a while - alone.'

She woke at four. She'd had another nightmare about the heckler. He had taken her to court for writing about him. He wanted half of all her earnings. Layla needed Mick to hold her, but he wasn't there. She'd been angry with him for not believing it was the same heckler in Leeds. As if she wouldn't know his voice by now. Layla could hear the heckler's voice all the time, awake or asleep. She needed more sleep. She stared at the ceiling for hours, then got up and tried to write. But she was too tired.

Chapter Seven

'Great news,' Ben said on the phone. 'You sold out the Albert Hall in a day.'

'What?' Layla asked.

'The last date on your tour. The Royal Albert Hall. We booked it last week, announced the show yesterday and sold out today. You're in the big time now.'

Layla had never even been to the Royal

Albert Hall. It was where they had the Last Night of the Proms. She knew the hall held over six thousand people. It was scary.

The crowd at Liverpool Empire were very friendly, but Layla was tired. She made some mistakes on the guitar and took too long tuning up between numbers. She almost deserved to be heckled. But nothing happened. The crowd applauded wildly, even though she was tired and sometimes sang flat.

'*Shouting at the Stars*,' someone yelled when she came back on to do the encore.

'I've not recorded that one yet,' Layla said. 'Some nights I feel like playing it and some I don't.'

'Go on,' the heckler yelled out. 'I don't mind.'

He was here. Layla took a deep breath. She knew what she had to do. Tonight

Layla wanted to keep the heckler talking. She needed Mick to see where he was.

'That's my most loyal fan,' Layla said to the crowd. 'You'll have to excuse him.'

'I don't need to be excused!' the heckler yelled.

'Maybe,' Layla said. 'But listen. I don't want you at any more of my gigs. It's not fair on me or anyone else.'

'Who said life was fair?' the heckler called out.

Mick should have found him by now. Layla sang the song. When it was over, she went straight into *Open Book*.

'Thank you,' she told the crowd. 'You've been lovely.'

Afterwards, she waited for Mick. He was nowhere to be seen. Their driver was missing too. She couldn't leave the Empire without them. Layla hoped that, at last, they had caught her heckler. She signed autographs for the fans who were waiting by the backstage door.

'You dealt with that heckler really well,' one fan told her.

'I'll bet he's mentally ill,' another said. 'We should feel sorry for him.'

'He might be ill, but that's no excuse,' the first fan said. 'He knows he's being horrible.'

Layla didn't comment. Mick and the driver returned after the last fan had left.

'What happened?' Layla asked. 'Did you find him?'

'We found him all right,' the driver said. 'We took him down to the docks.'

'What did you do to him?' Layla asked Mick.

'Put it this way,' Mick replied, 'he won't bother you again.'

Chapter Eight

It was the day of the Royal Albert Hall
concert. Layla couldn't sleep. She'd hardly
slept since Liverpool. She and Mick never
discussed exactly what happened in
Liverpool. She imagined the worst. Mick
would do anything for her. He had gone
too far.

Layla screamed. She had drifted into

sleep and there was the heckler. His body floated in the Mersey. A crab crawled out of his mouth.

Mick came in. He begged Layla to see the doctor.

'I get a week off after the Albert Hall,' Layla told him. 'A rest is all I need.'

'We could have a few days on an island somewhere,' Mick said.

'No, I want to go home to my family, my own room, alone. Sorry.'

'I understand,' Mick said, but he looked sulky. She had never thanked him for getting rid of the heckler. There had been no heckling at her shows since. Yet Layla had performed like a zombie. Each night, she was on stage for little more than an hour. People called out for *Shouting at the Stars* but she didn't sing it. She'd decided not to record it either. The song was cursed.

Her parents were coming tonight. They would take her home with them. A few nights in her own bed and she'd be fine. She'd do some festivals and record the vocal tracks for her second album. Then she'd take a long holiday. But not with Mick. After tonight's gig, she would tell Ben to let him go. She couldn't go out with a murderer.

'I'm glad you finally saw off that heckler,' Ben said before the show. 'He wasn't good for your image.'

'Is that all you're bothered about?' Layla asked. 'My image?'

'Maybe you should drop that song for a while,' Ben replied. 'Save it for the album after next.'

'I've already dropped it. If you'd been at my last few shows, you'd know that.'

'One more thing,' Ben said. 'Make sure you talk between songs. Tell a joke or two. Your songs might be miserable but you don't have to be. Mick says your last few shows have been very short. You can't do that here.'

'I'll do what I want,' Layla said. 'And, after tonight, I want a new bodyguard. A female one.'

'You want me to let Mick go?' Ben asked. 'I thought you and he were close.'

'You thought wrong!' Layla said. 'He doesn't suit my image. He doesn't suit me. Wait until after the show, then sack him.'

An hour later, she was on stage. The crowd gave her a standing ovation before she'd sung a note. Layla's throat was dry. She had to reach down for her water.

'Thank you so much,' she said, as the

crowd sat down. 'I don't know what to say, so I'd better sing.'

She found herself singing *Open Book*, even though she always saved it for last. The crowd applauded so wildly, she messed up and had to start the song again.

> *People see me, think they know me*
> *Tell me that I'm really strong*
> *Hard to take when words are fake*
> *Don't put your feelings in a song*
> *Keep them hidden, unforgiven*
> *Big words always come out wrong*
> *Thought I'd always be so lonely*
> *Then one day you came along*
>
> *Now my heart's an open book*
> *Take a look. Go on, take a look*

She finished the song without any mistakes. When the applause died down, Layla relaxed a little. She looked at the set list and tried to think of something funny to say.

'You wrote that song for me,' a voice called out. 'Even though you didn't know me then.'

It couldn't be him. Layla had seen blood on Mick's hands. She had seen the look in Mick's eyes. *He won't bother you again*, he'd promised. The heckler was dead.

'I didn't write that song for anyone,' Layla said.

'You wrote *Shouting at the Stars* for me. Don't deny it.'

'No, I didn't.'

There was nervous laughter from the crowd. It sounded like the heckler, but it must be a joker who had read about him. Layla didn't believe in ghosts. Best to ignore it.

'This is a song called *House on the Hill*,' she said, and began to sing.

The hall was so big, it was scary. Layla didn't feel like she was on stage. She felt like she was watching herself on television. TV often showed the audience here, waving flags and throwing balloons. It was like they were the show and she was the audience. And the heckler was out there, performing for her.

She forgot a few of the words and had to start one verse again, but got through the song. She started *Talking to No-one* straight away, so the heckler didn't get the chance to interrupt. She played it too fast, but never mind. The applause was less strong this time. Layla looked at the set list, tried to remember what song came next. The crowd went quiet.

'Aren't you going to sing *Shouting at the Stars?*' the heckler called out. 'Have you written a new last verse yet? You know, a verse where the star has the heckler murdered?'

'I didn't ask Mick to do that,' Layla said. 'I didn't mean it to go so far. Only, you wouldn't leave me alone.'

'You killed me!'

'I didn't.'

'You paid your bodyguard to do it!'

'I didn't know he'd kill you,' Layla pleaded. 'I asked him to warn you off, not murder you. I'm *not guilty*.'

Layla looked out into the audience. She wanted to see where the voice was coming from. It sounded so close. All she saw was Mick, running down the aisle, to help her. Ben appeared and stopped him. She watched the two men talk. After a moment, Mick walked away. Meanwhile, the crowd was restless. Layla heard talking. That was bad. She had to sing another song. Maybe she should do *Shouting at the Stars* one last time.

'This is about something bad that happened to me,' Layla said, but her voice didn't carry. Her mike wasn't working. She looked around to tell somebody there was a fault. Then she saw Ben walking to the front of the stage. He had a mike in his hand.

'That's all for tonight, folks. I'd like to apologise on Layla's behalf. She's been under a great deal of strain. We're very sorry. Keep your tickets and you'll get a full refund. Good night.'

He walked over to Layla and tried to pull her away from the mike. But her wheelchair lock was on and he didn't know how to turn it off.

'I didn't mean to do it!' Layla yelled. 'I didn't mean to have him killed!'

'No-one killed anyone,' Ben said, calmly.

'I've sent for the doctor.'

Ben left. Layla looked at the crowd. They were leaving quickly, politely, not speaking much. Then Ben returned. With him were her parents. Layla began to cry with relief.

'I'm sorry I let you down tonight,' Layla told her mum. 'When that guy started yelling, it freaked me out.'

'Nobody called out,' Mum said.

'Nobody?' Layla repeated.

'The doctor's on his way,' said Dad. 'There's nothing to worry about. We'll get you backstage.'

'Wait,' Layla said. She looked out at the empty seats. Only one person remained in the stalls. A young man in a woolly cap walked up the aisle. He walked slowly, using a stick. When he got to the front of the stalls, he stopped.

'Who are you?' Layla called out.

She knew the answer. She had seen him before, from a distance, in the crowd. Up close, she saw he was the guy in the photo on Mick's phone. She needed to know his story.

'Why do you do it?' she asked.

The heckler shook his head and pointed at his mouth.

His jaw was wired shut.

Look out for this exciting story
in the *Shades* series:

WITNESS

Anne Cassidy

Todd raised both his hands and gave the kid
an almighty shove so that he fell back on to
the pavement. Then, quick as a flash, Todd
squatted down, pushed the boy over and held
his arm up his back. The other kid was standing
still, holding the table leg up in the air.

'Touch me with that and I'll break his
arm,' Todd said.

The other kid looked like he might ignore
him so Todd pushed at the arm. Ripley gurgled
out some words and the other kid stepped
back and lowered the wood.

'Don't threaten me,' Todd said, 'I don't

grass on no one but your brother picked on an old man.'

With a last shove Todd stood up and watched as Ripley scrambled to his feet cradling his arm.

'You'll see me again, Lucas!' Ripley shouted, walking back to the car.

'Can't wait. Bring us a portion of chips next time!' said Todd.

The Ford drove off and Todd leaned back against the bus shelter. Louise moved up beside him. She linked her arm through his.

'You're shaking,' she said.

He shrugged. Then she planted a kiss on his cheek. He felt himself go red and hoped she didn't expect him to do anything in return.

The bus appeared. He gave Louise a weak smile as he stepped on. Inside he wasn't feeling good. Stephen Ripley. He would see him again, he was sure.